Edward Maslin Hulme

At Twilight

A Book of Lyrics

Edward Maslin Hulme

At Twilight
A Book of Lyrics

ISBN/EAN: 9783743324152

Manufactured in Europe, USA, Canada, Australia, Japa

Cover: Foto ©Andreas Hilbeck / pixelio.de

Manufactured and distributed by brebook publishing software
(www.brebook.com)

Edward Maslin Hulme

At Twilight

AT TWILIGHT

AT TWILIGHT
A BOOK OF LYRICS

BY

EDWARD MASLIN HULME

PREFATORY NOTE.

T HIS book of verse is scarcely more than a second
edition of my previous pamphlet, "An Evening
Thought." It has all been written during my un-
dergraduate course at Stanford University; and,
with a few exceptions, was printed in "The Sequoia,"
the University literary magazine. For the most
part it is reminiscent of my life in England, and
aims only to express different phases of a certain mood. The title was chosen for its suggestion
of the similarity of tone.

E. M. H.

Stanford University, California, May, 1897.

TO MY MOTHER,
ANNIE LOUISE HULME.

THERE is much that Time's lordship shall alter,
    Life's glory may dim with its rust,
Old loves and old memories shall falter,
    Old dreams shall be fallen to dust.
For the doom of all things earth-begotten
    Is to change as the flowers or the foam,
To fade as the grass, and, forgotten,
    In dust make their home.

The bright sword of Fame may be broken,
    The tower of Faith be thrown down,
Time's footsteps may leave their dim token
    Of dust on the sheen of Hope's crown.
Yet amid all the things that avail not,
    But pass as the foam of the sea,
Is thy love for me that shall fail not,
    And my love for thee.

CONTENTS.

AT TWILIGHT.

NEVER in the night or noon
   Come to me such thoughts of you
   As now, when in the deepening blue
Grows the glamour of the moon.

They are not born of vain regrets;
   Call it fancy or what you will,
   It is your eyes that I see still,
And not the purple violets.

Call it fancy or what you will,
   In the dreamy spell the twilight weaves
   I know I hear in the falling leaves
The sound of your footsteps, long since still.

AT SUNSET.

In the dim red glow of the sunset
  The tide is drifting home,
And the wide and desolate reaches
  Once more are a field of foam.

Upon the vanishing headland
  The red sun's last ray gleams,
While the deepening shadows are dancing
  The long day into dreams.

I hear a voice in the twilight
  That is calling low to me.
Is it one that comes from the windward,
  Out on the lonely sea?

Full of regret and desire,
  As your own heart used to be,
Do I hear your voice as I listen,
  Or the voice of my heart in me?

The wraith of the rain, in the shadows,
  Is haunting the shore we have known,
But, O, that it found me wandering
  With the twilight all my own.

EPHEMERA.

No month of summer with its poppied spell,
Though it be filled with sweetness as a shell
   Is filled with sound of the star-paven sea,
   May be as fair as that dear month to me,
When April's moon was our love's sentinel.

The orchard bloom against the silver shield
Of the clear sky was fair, and in the field
   Was heard the droning of the golden bee,
   The chamberer of each anemone
That was not fain its nectarous cup to yield.

That month of love hath fallen to dust and dreams;
The flower of all the years to me it seems;
   And yet it was of Time the ephemeron;
   Of Time who that dear month of love now done
No more than any withered flower esteems.

That silver note struck from Time's golden lute
Through all the lonely ages shall be mute,
   The string shall be unfingered; and to me
   The wandering wind shall be a threnody
Of that dear month at once both flower and fruit.

Time stayed not for thee then, nor for me now
He waits, this lord before whom Love must bow;
   He gathers every flower within his sheaves,
   And binds up all of them with poppy leaves,
And we are his ephemera, I and thou.

A TWILIGHT SONG.

WHEN swallows fly
　　On wistful wings,
And the rose-flushed sky
　　The darkness brings,—
Sing, shadowy pines,
　　Of the sail-winged sea,
And sing, O day,
　　Thy memory.

When the salt sea tide
　　Returns again,
O'er reaches wide,
　　With its sad refrain,—
Sing wailing tern,
　　The day forget,
To dreams return,
　　Leave old regret.

When ways to wander
　　Allure no more,
Stay wind to ponder
　　Beside my door,—
As some sea-shell
　　Sings of the sea
With its deep swell,
　　Sing thou to me.

When twilight falls,
　　And from afar
A lone thrush calls
　　The first pale star,—
Sing wind of the sha 'ows,
　　Sing wraith of the rain,
In the quiet meadows,
　　To me again.

QUESTIONING.

How mournful seems the autumn noon and long,
  How slow across the world the sun has drifted;
The dial since the lark's awakening song
  Hath scarcely shifted.

For naught of solace may my dreaming soul
  Find either in the morn or noontide golden;
But twilight bringeth thee, its aureole,
  By dusk enfolden.

So long the day hath been, a weary while;—
  Perchance it is as well, for then the dearer
Will be the wondrous grace of thy sweet smile,
  When thou art nearer.

All day I wait beneath the garden trees,
  And marvel where thy wandering feet are straying;
While wind-borne through the branches memories
  Are softly playing.

The autumn sun is warm; and ripe and fair
  The sun-red apples through the leaves are showing;
As though each fruit, thick-set and ruby, were
  A love-lamp glowing.

But down the garden-way with branches set
  There lie the leaves the dead spring hath begotten—
Ah, will my love, as we these leaves forget,
  Be e'er forgotten?

THE HOUSE OF DREAMS.

The Chambers of the House of Dreams.
                                    —Francis Thompson.

THERE is a chamber in the house of dreams
   That with a gentle loveliness is bright;
   There spectral lilies wind-unstirred are white,
While near the door the blood-red poppy gleams.
And with a wistfulness no other deems
   My heart through all the slow-winged hours of light
   Awaiteth at the postern gate of night,
Grown weary with the languorous noontide beams.

And all the magic of the chamber's spell
   The twilight beauty of thy heaven-blue eyes
Hath wrought. In speech grown almost audible
   They speak unto mine own with still replies.
Alone thou art the certain charm thereof,
For it is there thou dwellest, O my love!

REMEMBRANCE.

WHEN from the lilac bushes the evening winds have
  taken
 Their breath of dreamy odor, and when to song
  again
The golden-throated thrushes from drowsy noon
  awaken,
 And all the woods and meadows are sweet with
  April rain,

When soft in benediction the vesper bell is calling,
 And one pale star her taper is holding quietly,
While deep the twilight shadows upon the earth
  are falling,
 Within my heart arises the memory of thee.

AN EVENING THOUGHT.

Love, if some evening when the soft, white mist
   Holds in embracing arms the weary world,
And the last sunbeams all the peaks have kissed,
   And in sweet slumber all the flowers are furled,

You should come to me, clad in Death's dark grace,
   And gaze upon me with your tender eyes,
And with a sad, sweet smile upon your face,
   Should say, "I bring thee peace the world denies,"

Into the distant land I do not know,
   Into the darkness that I hope means light,
I would, dear heart, with you most gladly go,
   And you should be my guardian through the night.

THE VESPER CHIME.

Below the hills the westering sun is stealing,
    And lengthening shadows stir,
While mellowed sound of bells comes softly pealing
    Through far, dim fields of air.

Within my wistful heart there rise unbidden
    Thoughts far too deep for tears,
And one sweet face that is forever hidden,
    Fair as the bygone years.

It seems to me that in the twilight shadows
    The old glad days are here;
And, while one restless lark pipes in the meadows,
    I seem to feel you near.

But well I know no ecstasy of dreaming,
    Or vesper bell's refrain,
No matter how elusive be the seeming,
    Will bring you back again.

No more my grievous heart will be enraptured,
    As when, in days of old,
Your deepened eyes and soft hand held me captured,
    Between the dusk and gold.

Below the hills the westering sun is stealing,
    The stars come one by one,
While mellowed sound of bells are softly pealing,
    Orison, benison !

WHEN LOVE SHALL COME.

MY LOVE may come when swallows flit
  On wistful wings o'er lawn and lea,
When Spring a thousand lamps has lit
  In every cherry tree.

Or when through drowsy June-days long
  The sweet blue iris stars the stream,
When all the woods are filled with song,
  And pink wild-roses dream.

Or over crisp and yellow leaves
  My love may hold her rustling way,
When broad-wheeled wains with ripened sheaves
  Tell of the harvest day.

Or when the wandering rain and wind
  Go roaming o'er the far blue hills,
When lone swamp-robins pipe their thinned,
  Low, sorrow-shaken trills.

If she shall come in Spring, I fain
  Would wish the orchards April-kissed;
If Winter—let the wind and rain
  Go wandering where they list.'

For she alone can make the skies!
  I know when I shall hear her voice
The sun will shine from out her eyes,
  My longing heart rejoice.

LOVE'S GUERDON.

FROM distant reaches of the sky left bare,
 Unto the chamber of the urgent West,
 With pageant fitting for a royal guest,
To greater splendors that await him there,
The sun along a jeweled way doth fare;
 While in the trees the wind is manifest
 As one whose dreaming fingers, lightly press'd,
Make prelude to a song of twilight fair.

What dawn, or noon, or twilight, shall be mine
 To make the pilgrimage to unknown lands
 Not any omen known of man may say;—
 Only for me no splendid sunset way,
But in thy waiting eyes to see love shine,
 And feel again the pressure of thy hands.

Beneath the lilac tree,
  With its breathing blooms of white,
You waved a parting kiss to me
  In the deepening amber light.

Your face is always near,
  Your tender eyes of brown,
Sometimes in dreams again I hear
  The whisper of your gown.

Once more the lilac tree
  With twilight dew is wet,
And, O, I would that you might be
  Alive to love me yet.

MEMORIES.

SOMETIMES my thoughts go back again
   To where the sand-dunes, bleak and grey,
List to the sad sea's low refrain,
   And stretch to blue hills far away.

Where in the meadows of the dawn
   Full many a sky-lark sweetly sings,
With glad heart that the misty morn
   Such freshness and such joyance brings.

There where upon some headland steep,
   Amid the heather and the fern,
With white sea-dreams I fell asleep,
   Or listened to the wailing tern.

Where in the silence of the hills
   The murmur of the sea grows less,—
The memory of their silence fills
   Me with the old child-heartedness.

AUTUMN.

O AUTUMN, child of the fast-waning year,
  Of passionate desire and sad regret,
Whose tawny-coated thrushes, hushed in fear,
      No longer in the leafless twilight sing,
  Whose linnets all their morning lays forget,
      And wait in silence for the far-off spring,
  How like thee is my heart in sorrow set!

The twittering swallow's nest beneath the eaves
  Lies empty and forsaken; and afar
The idling fingers of the wind the leaves
      Have strewn along the roadside. As of old
  Thy footsteps on the painted hillsides are,
      But all thy wondrous charm, though wrought
          of gold,
  Has left my heart as cold as some pale star.   ·

When all the air was fragrant with the scent
  Of bean-fields far away and hawthorne tree,
Blithe-hearted through the woods and fields I went,
      Regarding April full of joyous moods,
  And all my heart was glad unspeakably,
      And comforted in leafy solitudes,
  With dreams that only feathered throats set free.

No more beside the clear and gentle stream
  The slim narcissus stores the morning rain,
And through the green and pleasant days to seem
      With wistful eyes to seek the wandering sun,
  Then watch the April twilight wax and wane.
      But now the wavering grace of spring is done,
  And none of all my idle dreams remain.

No more the woods are sweet with April rain;
  No more the bee goes wandering all the day
O'er hill and meadow, humming his blithe strain,
      To pillage orchard-blossoms and the shrines
  Of primroses that by the roadside sway;
      And all the world, except the shadowy pines,
  Is steeped in the deep pathos of decay.

For now the leaves lie where of late they threw
  Their grateful shadows on the April lea.
Beneath the reaches of the austere blue,
      O'er all the pensive autumn world there lowers,
  Arrayed in all his autumn sorcery,
      Death; and fair April, with her fragrant flowers,
  Has yielded long ago to what must be.

FANTASY.

Dim are her sea-grey eyes, and, amber-tressed,
    Her brows are fair;
As white as ivory newly sawn her breast
    Is gleaming bare;
And wandering slowly down the garden-way
    I see her pass.
The moon is wan, and soft the low winds sway
    The creeping grass.

So sad and strange there comes a serenade,
    A lingering sigh,
A plaintive tinkling that her fingers played
    In years gone by.
So sad upon the air that sweet old tune
    It floats along,
And fills the garden, lit by the pale moon,
    With lonely song.

And ever in the dusk, when day grows old,
    I wait for her;
When soft and slow night cometh, shadowy-stoled,
    And all is fair.
How sweet in this dim moonlit night in May
    The fallen rain
Hath left the roses where she held her way,
    But all in vain!

However fair, no earthly odors blown,
    However sweet,
Or ruby glow of any love-lamp shown,
    May stay her feet.
What joys foregone, what earthly fate foresworn,
    Arise in her,
That, 'mid the asphodels beyond the bourn,
    She may not fare?

IN THE CONVENT GARDEN.

WITHIN the convent garden, at the dusk
    Of day, when the pale yellow primrose blows,
And mignonette and violets and musk
    Make fragrant all the garden's sweet repose,

Near where a wild-rose, trained along the wall
    Of mossy stones, lets blossoms pink and sweet
In tangled masses through a crevice fall,
    A nun reclines upon a carvèd seat.

Her long white robes just touch the lavender
    That borders all the pathways, which the breeze
Has carpeted with petals pale and fair,
    Blown like a petal snow from almond trees.

And through the garden's hush there comes the song
    Of two gold-throated nightingales who seem
To sing their hearts out all the evening long,
    Near where the roses on the old wall dream.

Fair nun, in these days of a restless age,
    Within thy garden of sweet, fragrant bloom,
I envy thee thy simple heritage,
    Thy life that ne'er is shadowed with doubt's gloom.

THE END OF DAY.

THE twilight falls, and the breezes,
    Over the valleys and hills,
Are bearing a faint remembrance
    Of a dead spring's daffodils.

Far over the purple heather,
    As in days of the bygone time,
The cathedral bells are sounding
    The self-same vesper chime.

They bear the same old message,
    But for you no more they beat
The passing of the hours,
    So sad, and solemn, and sweet.

I wait through shine and shadow
    For the time when I shall greet
Your sweet blue eyes so tender,
    Where the song and the silence meet.

MY SEA.

STILLED is the fervent rapture that was mine
   When as a child my soul thy strange spell knew,
When stars were paling, or at day's decline,
   Yet has my heart to thee been leal and true.

It was a tremulous ecstasy to stray
   Along thy shore in a child's dream of thee,
And listen to thy winds by night or day,
   What message from afar they brought to me.

Oft have I cried to thee in lonely need,
   Being but a child and full of fear;
And thou hast ever harkened and gave heed,
   Until my heart knew that thy heart was near.

In this far summer land I dwell apart,
   And sigh for thy perforced relinquished ways.
I walk forlorn and weary, and my heart
   Is full of unforgotten yesterdays.

I know that when the world is full of sleep
   And weariness of life and love for me,
That I shall hear thy voice: thy lone shores keep
   For me an ever-ready hostelry.

A MEMORY.

Where jasmine grows beside the door
   She stood, unconscious of her grace,
With all the sunlight streaming o'er
     Her pretty face.

I can recall her very look;
   Her eyes, from out their tenderness
An air, it seemed, the whole world took
     Of gentleness.

LILACS.

From many slender, feathered throats
Come sweet, delicious, limpid notes;
    Along the gust-sweet garden-way
    The lilac bush is gay.

The nightingale sings to the rose
In many a moonlit garden-close;
    Thy lover is no lyric bird:
    A moth thy heart has stirred.

A moth whom from thy fragrant lips
So charily the nectar sips,
    Who, 'neath the trembling stars above,
    Murmurs his word of love.

Teach me thy charm, O happy flower,
That lures a lover in an hour
    Of lessening light, that so may I
    My love keep ever nigh. ,

NOCTURNE.

A FRAGRANCE comes from the garden,
   Where roses and violets grow,
As it came in the tender twilight
   Of an evening long ago.

And far through the shadowy pine trees
   Comes floating a vesper chime,
To me as I sit in the twilight,
   And dream of the olden time.

And it seems to me while waiting,
   In the hush of the sweet spring night,
That I hear the voice of my darling,
   See the gleam of her eyes so bright.

Is it only a bird that is singing
   Above on the jasmine spray?
Is it only the stars that are shining
   In the waning of the day?

IN THE QUADRANGLE.

MORNING IN AUTUMN.

The warmful rays of the autumnal sun
   Shine bright upon the red-tiled roofs and towers;
   Where up the wall there climb the jasmine flowers
Rose-breasted birds are calling one by one;
The trustful sparrows, not to be outdone,
   Unceasing chatter through the morning hours;
   And, having left to winter's ruinous powers
Their nests, the pilgrim swallows all are gone.

And like the swallows I shall soon depart
   From thee, beloved court, to other ways,
   Bearing through time thy many yesterdays,
Made passional and influent, in my heart:—
   Not knowing if the future shall see all
   My boyish dreams to dust and ashes fall.

Stanford University.

34

IN THE QUADRANGLE.

EVENING IN SUMMER.

How beauteous in the moonlight seem the long
   Arcades and court, where in the busy day
   So many hurried feet have held their way,
And bright and eager youthful faces throng!
Through the all-golden afternoon the song
   Was heard of birds with joy of summer gay;
   But ere the advent of the moony ray
They sought their nests deep-throated blooms among.

Softly the saintly light is falling down;
   The sweet and solemn beauty of the hour,
Of all the summer day the very crown,
   When sleepeth every bird and every flower;—
This is an hour, O heart, for thee to save
To give a beauty to thine inmost cave.

Stanford University.

AT LENTEN VESPERS.

Through leafless trees the evening sun shines red,
   And flushes with its momentary glory
The great Cathedral pane whereon is spread
   A saintly story.

The graceful image of Our Lady stands
   Amid tall lilies in the yellow lustre;
While worshipers devout with folded hands
   Around her cluster.

The priests in penitential violet clad
   Waft incense upward in a wavering column;
While from the choir there steals a hymn so sad,
   So soft, and solemn.

The wondrous mystery of worship there
   Is held in vague and tremulous possession,
Then wafted on the taper-lighted air
   In sweet expression.

What though my soul at last is reft of fears!
   Assured of mind, there still arise within me
Dim longings for the unforgotten years
   That yet would win me.

THE PASSING OF LOVE.

WHERE sweet the tender peach-blooms blow,
  Along the garden wall,
She sat and waited through the day
  For the sound of Love's footfall.

She said: "He seeks me over the world,
  He seeks me the whole year through;
But surely, to-day, that I wait for him,
  He will find me, my lover true.

"I shall not say that I wait for him,
  And the light in his deepening eyes,
As his heart is filled with a nameless joy,
  I shall greet with a feigned surprise."

She laughed and sang through the April morn;
  She played through the noontime still;
But at last there crept a fear in her heart,
  And she sighed in the twilight chill.

Then a small voice whispered within her heart,
  As the westering sun sank low,
That Love, unheeded, had passed that way,
  In the morning, long ago.

SUPPLICATION.

THE wind is heavy with roses,
    And the lambent, ruby blaze
Of the silver lamp discloses
    A chalice of chrysoprase.

I have placed it upon thine altar,
    Aphrodite, goddess so fair,
But my fainting lips they falter,
    As I utter to thee my prayer.

From the pearly shell that is shaken
    By the winds on thy moony sea,
Ah! who is the one that hath taken
    The secrets known to thee?

From the trembling words that are spoken,
    Ah, who can tell what abides
In my heart? They are but the token
    Of the sorrow that there resides.

A lover, whose charm encloses
    The whole of my sorrowing life,
Came ere the radiant roses,
    The rich red roses, were rife.

We talked in those bygone hours
    Of the days that were to be;—
Fate filled our folded flowers
    With thorns we could not see.

For now in death he reposes
    In some misty cave of thine,
Where the depth of the dim sea closes
    The changes of sound and shine.

Far over the weary water,
    Where the wan light wanes in the west,
Take me, Aphrodite, thy daughter,
    And lay me with him at rest.

The wind is heavy with roses,
    And the lambent, ruby blaze
Of the silver lamp discloses
    A chalice of chrysoprase.

I have placed it upon thine altar,
    Aphrodite, goddess so fair;
But my fainting lips they falter,
    As I utter to thee my prayer.

LOVE'S ADVENT.

It may be that before the winds
Are filled by summer with the scent
　Of roses, and before the thrill
　Of life has stirred the trees until
Their leaves a deeper shade have lent
　Unto the sloping orchard hill.

Or it may be when through the air
The yellow butterflies and bees,
　O'er meadows and by woodland ways,
　Go foraging in summer days;
When summer's spell is on the seas,
　And every sailing shadow stays.

It matters not what time it is,
If blue or grey be all the skies,
　If spring or summer-time be here,
　For me at least when Love is near
The sun will shine from out her eyes,
　And banish every waiting fear.

A GENTIAN.

SWEET little flower of autumn skies,
  The sun his golden wealth on thee
Sheds not; and yet thy sapphire eyes
  Are matchless in their purity.

The roses' gaudy loveliness
  Speaks ill the message of thy flower:
They, with their flaunting crimson dress,
  Come only in a summer hour.

Ah! great thine honor thus to grow,
  And in thy message never err,
And rich the blessing 'tis to know
  Thou art God's silent chorister.

For as I pluck thee tenderly
  From where thou grow'st in the sod,
I think, sweet flower, if but for thee
  That I should know there is a God.

A LINNET RHAPSODY.

B ENEATH the overhanging trees,
   Along the iris-bordered stream,
And where, in passing, every breeze
   Speaks to the roses as they dream,

And pauses lightly to caress
   The lady-ferns, whose fragile ways,
So ærial is their slenderness,
   Seemed fashioned but for fairies' gaze,

There where the linnets sing unseen,
   With liquid, purling, silvery notes,
Amid the foliage, dense and green,
   From out their little golden throats,

I lie, and in their music sweet
   Forget that things must cease to be,
Forget that joys are incomplete,
   In their melodious rhapsody.

SILENTLY, softly,
  Come when you will—
In nectarous noon,
Or exquisite eve,
Or midst of the night when the musk-rose sleeps—
As still as the scent
Of a fragile flower.

> Silently, softly,
> Come when you will,
> When dark are the days
> 'Neath shadowy skies,
> And I am tired of the weary way—
> As still as the leaf
> That floats on a stream.

Silently, softly,
Come when you will,
And over the Sea-
Of-the-Silent-Spell
That shows no sail let us sail away
To the distant shore that sends no sound.

BALLADE OF THE WATERS OF ACHERON.

Upon a shore, alone, within the gloom
　　By moon or stars unlit, I hear the strain
Of listless waters lapping, that resume
　　With added woe the wild and strange refrain
　　Of voices of gaunt spectres who complain,
While force unseen, unceasing bears them on.
　　Where go these ghosts, I ask again, again,
Across the waters of dread Acheron?

The constant murmur of the sea's dull boom
　　Has filled my heart with languor and with pain.
Bound for the depths of yonder vast sea-room
　　Has one soul of those dead men chanced to gain
　　Aught from his past exultant years? In vain
I ask again; no answer falls upon
　　Mine ears. To what place leads life's lane
Across the waters of dread Acheron?

Charon in shadowy robes I see assume
　　Command of the strange craft that sails the main,
Trackless and drear, whose verge will soon consume
　　Those ghostly forms who go where long has lain
　　The awful secret men for ages fain
Have been to learn the answer if, though vain. Is done
　　Their phantom journey when they reach the plain
Across the waters of dread Acheron?

ENVOY.

Spirit, whose hand doth hold our life's frail chain,
Is it for weary mortals to attain
　　To some far land where day and night are one
　　Across the waters of dread Acheron?

AT THE BALL.

THERE are many feet in their satin shoes that lightly
    glance and go,
There are many eyes beneath the light that joy-
    ously flash and glow,
But of all the eyes that gleam in the dance there
    are only two that I know.

O wondrous fair is the golden star, the star of the
    morning skies,
And fair is the tender flower of blue that blossoms
    when April dies,
But fairer than flower and star of the dawn is the
    light in her sweet blue eyes.

She sits in the corner and chats with one, a hand-
    some young fellow she knows,
And sways her delicate satin fan with its Cupids *en
couleur de rose,*
And smiles, as she never has smiled on me, at his
    carelessly dropped *bon mots.*

But once in the dance there came to me a golden
    hour of hours,
Whose glamour and sweetness forever regret and
    joy in my heart empowers,
When once we met and my dreaming heart was
    filled with the scent of her flowers.

There are many feet in their satin shoes that lightly
    glance and go,
There are many eyes beneath the light that joy-
    ously gleam and glow,
But of all the eyes that gleam in the dance there are
    only two that I know.

O wondrous fair is the golden star, the star of the
    morning skies,
And fair is the tender flower of blue that blossoms
    when April dies,
But fairer than flower and star of the dawn is the
    light in her sweet blue eyes.

A HEART-SONG.

I WILL tie my heart to the petal
  Of a lily's pure, white bell,
And when the night-wind swings it
  The song of my heart shall swell,

To where my love lies dreaming
  Under the wild-rose tree,
And she will know that the breezes
  Are bearing a message from me.

HERE in the distant clime, where the yellow poppies
    in springtime
Cover the valleys and hills with their shimmering
    golden clusters,   ·
Builded the monks of old, the monks from the
    Spanish cloisters.
What of their work remains, of the long arcades
    and the bell-towers,
Only the fragment here of a pillar with vines en-
    ·twinèd,
Of a pillar all quaintly carved with many a curious
    fretwork,
Now almost obscured by the thickly growing
    lichen,
That has caught and held the color of the golden
    haze of the noontime?
Naught of the red-tiled roof, or the rafters made of
    the redwood,
Made of the odorous redwood, brought from the
    mountain cañons,
There where in deepest shadows the ferns grow tall
    and delicate,
And where the sweet spring waters gush from their
    wells that are mossy?
What of their work remains; only the graven
    tombstones
Set in the fragrant bloom that grows in the south-
    ern valleys,
Marking the place where the monks their last long
    rest are taking?
Do you seek the remains of their work? Not here
    in the lonely pillar;
Nor there in the bloom-covered graves. Go search
    in the lives of the people.

Something, I doubt not, remains of the work of the
    monks of the old-time.
Down through the years it has come, though per-
    haps we may not discern it.
Just as the spring's clear waters are held in the
    swift flowing river,
So the result of their work, of their every noble en-
    deavor,
Is found in the lives of the people who live in the
    sun-kissed valleys,
Where in the years gone by the monks from the
    Spanish cloisters
Builded the long arcades with the red-tiled roofs
    and the bell-towers.